Teacup House

The Twitches Bake a Cake

By **Hayley Scott**   Illustrated by **Pippa Curnick**

Chapter One
Party Time

Stevie Gillespie was precisely 117.6 centimetres tall, with long brown hair that she wore in a big plait on one side of her head. She had it on the side so she could twirl it between her fingers when she was thinking.

Today, Stevie was at the kitchen counter, kneeling on one of the dining chairs. She was mixing edible, bright-purple glitter into a huge bowl of butter icing.

She twisted the spoon this way and that. She was so excited to be helping Mum ice the big purple cake for their moving-in party.

Stevie was thinking about everything
that had happened this very busy week:

1. She and Mum moved from
    the city to the country, and it
    turned out Stevie loved it.

2. Nanny Blue gave
    Stevie a teacup
    house and
    its little family of
    toy rabbits,
    the Twitches.

3. Stevie lost
    the daddy
    rabbit,
    Gabriel Twitch.

Gabriel.

4. Stevie found him again.

Phew!

After spending most of their moving-in day looking for Gabriel in the garden, he'd somehow turned up in her bedroom with the other Twitches, Bo, Silver and Fig.

Bo.   Silver.   Fig.

Relieved and excited, Stevie had spent the past few days carefully arranging, and rearranging, all the Twitches's belongings, until she'd got the inside of the teacup house looking just right.

Now it sat on the kitchen counter in its pretty saucer garden. She loved the house's tiny blue tiles and the delicate painted ivy that crept along the walls. She loved the tiny little flowers that sat in the cheerful red window boxes, and the little sign swinging above the blue front door. And most of all, she loved the four

Twitches: Bo, Gabriel, Silver and
Fig. They really were the most
delightful little toy rabbits you could
possibly imagine.

Today, she'd set them up as
though they were doing work
in the garden.

"Yum yum, hey, Twitches!" Stevie said, as she took a lick of the icing from a thick dollop on the back of the wooden spoon. "I think the icing's ready, Mum, and it's delicious!"

Stevie winked at the four rabbits and looked at the giant four-layer cake Mum had made for the moving-in party that she'd organized specially to introduce them to their new neighbours. Though

Mum had made lots of tasty party treats, Stevie was looking forward to tucking into the purple party cake most of all.

"Good," said Mum. "It's nearly one o'clock, and the party starts in half an hour. It's time to ice the cake."

Whenever Stevie thought about the party she felt nervous. She liked parties, she really did. But she could be what grown-ups wrongly called "shy" and what Stevie called, "taking my time to get to know people in my own way".

Getting to know people was one of

her biggest worries about moving to the country. What if nobody liked her? What if she didn't make any friends at all?

Stevie tried not to worry, and went and grabbed two spatulas instead. Together, she and her mum spread thick swirls of sparkly purple icing all over the cake, before smoothing it down so it looked neat and yummy.

"Nice work," said Mum, beaming as she handed Stevie a tub of little silver balls for her to decorate the cake with. There were loads of them.

She tried to spread them out as

neatly as possible, telling herself she'd
enjoy the party. Why wouldn't she?

And, yes she was worried,
and yes she was nervous, but as always
she'd try her best.

She wasn't going
to let today be
anything less
than brilliant.

 Chapter Two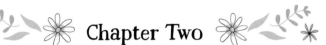
Rabbits Make a Plan

Stevie pulled her concentration face
as she held an icing bag between her
hands and piped a big purple flower
on top of the cake, just like Mum had
taught her.

As the flower started to take shape,
Stevie wondered who would be at the
party. They didn't know anybody in the
countryside yet, other than Dad and

Stuart. They only lived two miles away on their farm, but they couldn't come because they had something very important they had to do with their cows.

"That's really brilliant," said Mum, beaming as Stevie finished her iced flower.

Stevie felt proud of herself. "And,"
Mum continued, "there's somebody
coming up the garden path who I think
would very much like to see you."

Stevie looked up, her heart beating
fast. "Who?"

Mum paused, then smiled. "Nanny
Blue."

"Nanny Blue!" Stevie exclaimed.
Nanny Blue was Stevie's Favourite
Person (who wasn't Mum or Dad) and
she hadn't seen her for a whole week.
Stevie picked up Bo and Gabriel from
the saucer garden and put them in her
pocket with the yellow star. She wanted

to show Nanny Blue the new little jackets she'd made them from one of Mum's old scarves and some yellow ribbon. Before Mum could tell Stevie to put on some shoes, she had opened the kitchen door and run off into the garden.

As soon as the coast was clear, Fig
and Silver Twitch looked at each other
and wiggled their noses with delight.

"Quick! Let's go out and take a
closer look!" said Silver excitedly.

"Have you seen that amazing glittery
icing on the cake?" said Fig, pointing to
the other side of the kitchen counter.

Despite having a felt carrot attached
to his hand, he hated carrots. But he
loved cake. And icing!

"Do you think we could find a way to taste some?" he said. "Maybe a tiny nibble, from the side?"

"It does look delicious," said Silver, the start of an idea sparking in her head. "I think we should make our own – a lovely surprise cake for when Mama Bo and Daddy Gabriel get back." Ever since their first day at the cottage, Silver had been wondering what adventures she could have next.

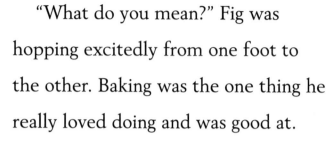

"What do you mean?" Fig was hopping excitedly from one foot to the other. Baking was the one thing he really loved doing and was good at.

"I mean, we've got all the ingredients to make a cake here in the teacup house," said Silver. "And you can show me how. But, to make it extra special, we could get some of that sparkly purple icing and put it on our cake. Imagine what it would look like!"

Fig's face lit up, then he frowned.

"Won't Mama Bo and Daddy Gabriel be cross if we leave the teacup house by ourselves, especially without asking first?"

"But they're not here to ask, are they?" said Silver, twitching her nose and grinning with mischief. "And besides, everybody loves surprises. And cake! So, are you with me?"

Fig looked at the thick icing, sparkling and purple in the huge bowl in the not too far distance.

"Yes," he said. "I definitely am."

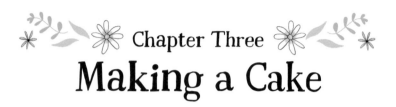

Chapter Three
Making a Cake

In the garden Stevie rushed at Nanny
Blue so hard that she nearly knocked
her over. Stevie had never squeezed
anybody so tightly in her life. Nanny Blue
squeezed her just as hard, right back.

"Stevie!" she said.

"Nanny Blue! I've missed you!" Stevie
didn't let go.

"It's only been a week," said Nanny
Blue, but she had tears in her eyes.

"It's been ages," said Stevie.

"Tell me what you've been up to," said Nanny Blue, kissing Stevie on her head.

Stevie started talking very fast about all the things that had happened since they'd moved to the country, as she pulled on the rainbow boots that Mum had brought down the garden. Nanny Blue and Mum smiled at each other.

Inside the cottage Silver and Fig had hopped inside the teacup house to the study, where all the little Twitch books were kept on the wooden bookshelves. They needed to find a

recipe for a really
big cake.

   "Let me see…"
said Fig, who was
the baking expert.
"Here we are.
*Baking for
Bunnies.*"

He pulled a thick hardback book down from the shelves. Inside there were pages of cupcakes, chocolate cakes, tower cakes, stacked cakes, cream puff pie cakes and buns. Then, on page 73, there it was. The cake. The Purple Party Cake of Fig's dreams, a huge cake covered in lots of thick purple icing.

Silver and Fig looked at each other, then back at the picture of the cake. It was perfect.

Giant Purple Party Cake

This four-tier purple party cake is sure to wow any bunny — and it is yummy!

Cut a circle of baking parchment to fit the bottom of your baking tins.

Cream the butter and sugar together until pale. Beat in eggs.

Sift in the flour and fold in using a large metal spoon.

For the icing, see recipe on p183, and whisk all the ingredients together.

Use a s
Move the
rest of the
Scrape into

Bake for 20 minutes. Test with a skewer to make sure cooked. Leave for 5 minutes. Turn the cake onto a wire rack. Wash and dry the tin.

Fig wrote down all the things they needed on a piece of paper. He put a tick next to the ones they already had.

✓ Flour

✓ Eggs

✓ Butter

✓ Caster sugar

✓ Food colouring

Icing – SEE rECiPE ON PagE 183

"Right," he said. "So, we just need that purple icing to make our cake really special."

They looked at each other, buzzing
with excitement.

"It doesn't take long to make a
cake," Fig said. "Let's mix it up now
and get it in the oven, whilst we work
out how to get the icing. You find the
cake tins and line them with
greaseproof paper, and I'll measure
everything out."

"Right, chef!" said
Silver doing a salute.
They both laughed.
Before long Fig
was whisking all
the ingredients
up in a big bowl,

and Silver had
lined four tins to
make the different
layers of the cake.
Silver poured
the mixture
into each of

the four tins. "Right,"
he said, turning
the dial on the
little oven.
"Time to
pop them in
to bake."

Fig licked the mixture from his
whisk and took a deep, happy sigh.

He and Silver stared out of their
kitchen window at all the giant plates
covered with cling film. Carefully,
they crept out of the back door of the
teacup house to look at all the
delicious food. Everything was SO BIG.

There were sausage rolls, sandwiches,
curly crisps, straight crisps and crisps
that looked like animal paw prints.
There were pretty rainbow cupcakes,
and fruit in a huge bowl; oranges,
bananas, grapes, melon.

And of course there was the giant
purple cake all the way round the
other side of the counter.

Silver gazed out as she thought
really hard about how to get round to
the other side of the counter without
being seen.

Suddenly there was a voice
at the door to the kitchen
and Silver and Fig
Twitch froze.

It was Mum,
Stevie and
Nanny Blue.
They came
into the
kitchen and
took jugs of
squash and
lemonade,
paper cups
and two big
bowls of crisps,
then went back out into the garden.

"Phew, that was close," Fig
exclaimed. "We nearly got caught then."

"I've got it!" said Silver. "We need to make ourselves disguises."

"We do?" said Fig, licking some cake mix off his carrot. "How about some spectacles? Or a moustache? I've always wanted a moustache."

"Maybe," giggled Silver. "I have other ideas!"

Chapter Four
A Clever Plan

"I want to show Nanny Blue the plants in the teacup house garden," said Stevie. "And I want to show her my ideas for Silver and Fig's new jackets."

"Well, there'll be plenty of time for that after the party," said Mum, balancing a stack of paper cups in one arm and holding a jug of squash in the other.

"Come on, Stevie," said
Nanny Blue, as they walked
down the garden. "The first
guests are here."

Stevie could see two grown-ups she
didn't know, and a girl who must have
been about her age, in a bright yellow
dress, leggings and
bright green roller
skates. The girl
was frowning.
The woman
was carrying
a baby and a
bunch of
flowers, and
the man
carried a box of
strawberries.

Stevie and the girl eyed each other suspiciously. The girl frowned and looked down at her roller skates.

Stevie's heart sank. Even though she'd had lovely friends in the city, there had been some girls at her old school who were not very nice to her. They'd told her that her hair looked silly, and teased her for doing gardening.

They used to frown like that too,
before they said mean things and
turned away, or pushed her and left her
with nobody to play with.

"Say hello," said Mum
enthusiastically. "This is Osa and Zak."
She pointed at the grown-ups. "And
this is Eshe – who's in the same year as

you at school – and her little sister, Maya. They live next door, and I think you're going to be great friends."

Everybody other than Eshe said, "Hello."

"Osa and I were saying only last night," said Mum to Nanny Blue, "how lovely it will be for the girls to have someone their own age living next door."

"We've already planned to take it in turns to pick them both up when the other is working," said Osa. "The girls will be able to play after school. It's perfect."

Stevie and Eshe stared at each other.

Playing after school? Pick-ups? From the look on Eshe's face, she agreed with Stevie on one thing. It was no fun having grown-ups make decisions about your life without even asking.

At that very moment, in the kitchen, Silver and Fig stood at the edge of the counter. It was going to be tricky to get all the way round, especially with people coming and going in the kitchen.

"So, what's the disguise?" asked Fig.

Silver looked
about her. The
straws were too
narrow to hide
behind or inside.
The napkins would
look too bumpy if they
put them over their heads.

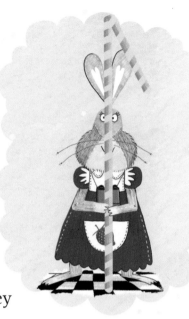

Then she saw
the pretty,
coloured stack
of cupcake cases
next to a plate
of sausage rolls.

"Aha!" she said jumping with delight.
"We could use those."

Fig looked at the cases. He imagined hiding under them like they were little tortoises when people came in, and it made him laugh with joy. "Yes!" he said. "Yes, yes, yes! I think it might work!"

"We've got twenty-five minutes, right?" asked Silver.

"Twenty-one now," said Fig, checking the giant wall clock. He knew how important it was to take the cakes out of the oven at the right time

"Right," said Silver. "My plan is this. We empty our biscuit jar, and put it in my backpack so we have somewhere to store the icing. Let's share a cupcake case, so we're less obvious. We'll need to be careful as we journey between the party food mountains, and drop our cake case over our heads, crouch down and keep still if anyone comes in."

"It sounds like it could work," said Fig, already thinking how good that sparkly icing would look on their purple surprise cake.

"Of course it does," said Silver, tipping the biscuits from the big glass jar onto the table. "What could possibly go wrong?"

Chapter Five
Falling Down

In the garden more guests were arriving from the village, all with children much younger than Stevie. Mum was pouring drinks into brightly coloured paper cups and chatting happily. Mum had told Stevie to talk to Eshe, but Eshe was rolling her feet back and forth in her shiny green roller skates and pretending Stevie didn't exist.

Nanny Blue had started making

balloon animals.
The other
children were
watching her and
giggling as she
produced
balloon
giraffes and
mermaids
and pirates.
Stevie wanted
to join in but
she didn't
know how.

She wished Dad and Stuart had come to the party. She had no one to talk to.

Stevie took a side glance at Eshe, who at exactly the same moment took a side glance at her. She had to admit that Eshe's roller skates were really very excellent.

Stevie wanted to say something like:

1) I think your roller skates are really beautiful. I like green too.

2) What's your school like?

3) Do you like having a baby sister?

4) You're not going to be mean and push me around, are you?

But still she didn't say anything.

Instead she took Mama Bo and
Daddy Gabriel out of her pocket. She
stroked their little ears, and bounced
them up and down on the grass in front
of her. Stevie was busy playing when
several things happened at once.

1. A small child popped his balloon mermaid and it made an almighty

BANG!

2. Maya started crying, very loudly.

3. One of the other children ran, scared, right into Nanny Blue's legs.

4. Nanny Blue took a big fall.

At first people laughed. It looked like it was part of her performance with the balloons as she had been making jokes and being silly. But when Nanny Blue didn't get up straight away, Stevie rushed over to her to see if she was okay.

To her surprise, Eshe had already skated over. Her new neighbour was kneeling on the grass, holding Nanny Blue's hand.

"Nanny!" said Stevie. "Are you okay?"

Nanny Blue was shaking. She had a big bump forming by her elbow, all red and swollen.

Stevie's mum came rushing back up the garden. "Are you okay?" Mum looked really panicky and scared, and Stevie knew how she felt because it was a shock to see Nanny Blue hurt. "Do I need to call an ambulance?"

"An ambulance!" Nanny Blue said

loudly, a smile starting to spread across her face. "Don't be so ridiculous. All I did was get myself a little bump. I'm totally fine." She went to stand up but was a bit wobbly on her feet. Eshe was still holding her other arm.

"Stevie," said Mum, "would you go and fetch some ice from the freezer? Nanny's got a nasty bump on her arm. We need to stop the swelling."

Stevie nodded, before scooping up Bo and Gabriel Twitch, popping them in her pocket and running towards the house. She was thinking four things.

1. Was Nanny Blue really okay?
2. She really, really loved Nanny Blue.
3. Why had Eshe rushed to help her?
4. If Eshe was being kind to Nanny Blue, maybe she wasn't mean after all...

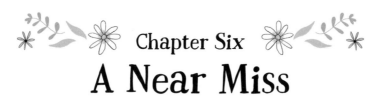

Chapter Six
A Near Miss

In the kitchen, Silver and Fig chose a cupcake case. It was a lovely light blue with white spots on it, and perfectly sized to cover them both. Giggling, but nervous, they held the cake case over their heads with a cocktail stick, like a little paper umbrella. Silver had the backpack with the biscuit jar inside firmly strapped to her shoulders as, together, the two rabbits began their

journey through the huge party-food landscape. There were the plates of sliced peppers and carrots, and cut cucumbers that were stacked high like logs.

Then a huge wad of napkins, all in

different colours, that looked like a big

bed, covered in lovely blankets. They

walked as quickly as they could, trying

not to trip over anything. When Fig

accidentally bashed his bottom into the

edge of the napkins, they began to wobble.

"Careful!" said Silver. "You don't want that lot falling down on you!"

Just as she said that, one of the napkins tumbled onto the counter, narrowly missing them. The rabbits looked at each other nervously and kept moving forward. Next they came across a huge potato covered in silver foil and pinpricked with cocktail sticks tipped with chunks of cheese and pineapple. From where Silver and Fig were standing the whole thing looked like some magical metal tree with yellow leaves, and for a moment they forgot what they were supposed to be doing.

"Wow!" said Silver.

"Wow!" said Fig.

Next, Stevie's mum had left out a plate of butter for people to put on baguettes. Fig was standing right next to it. All he could see were huge curls of shiny, yellow butter. It looked so golden, like a big dollop of sunshine. Surely it wouldn't hurt if he had a little taste? Quickly, Fig pushed his paw right into the curls of butter and squished it about. It felt warm and gooey and really splendid.

Just as he was about to pull his paw out to lick off all the butter, Stevie came bursting into the kitchen to find some ice for Nanny Blue's bump. Silver pulled their cocktail stick to the ground immediately, but Fig's arm was still in the butter. Even though the cupcake case was upside down and the two rabbits were under it, it didn't sit flat. If you looked carefully, you'd see his little arm between the edge of the case and the edge of the butter.

"Fig!" Silver mouthed crossly. "What are you doing?"

"I don't know!" said Fig, unsure whether to slide his arm out and under their cake case, risking Stevie seeing or hearing it move, or to leave it there and hope for the best.

Silver lifted up the edge of the cake case so she could see what was happening. Stevie was clattering about with a bowl, the ice-cube tray, and a tea towel.

As the two Twitches huddled down under their cupcake case, they couldn't help but wonder if venturing out of the teacup house had been a terrible mistake.

Stevie could turn and spot them at any moment. What would they do if she saw them?

Stevie was refilling the empty ice-cube tray with water, ready to put it back into the freezer.

Phew, thought Silver. *She'll be gone in a minute.* Just as she thought that, Stevie turned suddenly and looked directly at them. Not only that, but Mama Bo and Papa Gabriel's heads were poking out of Stevie's pocket. Mama Bo caught Silver's eye. She didn't look very pleased at all.

"Mmm, butter," said Stevie, taking a step towards them. Silver and Fig started to tremble. Silver held her breath. Fig's arm was still squelched into the butter.

Suddenly, Stevie's huge hand came looming down above the cake case. Silver squeezed her eyes shut as Fig stifled a tiny squeal. There was nothing they could do. Stevie had seen them. The game was up.

Chapter Seven
Quick, Run!

Stevie reached down to stick her finger
into the thick curls of butter. How she
loved the taste of it. She pushed her
finger into the yellow goo, accidentally
brushing her hand against Silver and
Fig's cupcake case so that it wobbled
from side to side, and nearly tipped
over. Stevie put her fingers into her
mouth and licked the butter off, then
reached down again. Her hand came
so near to Fig, he could almost feel

the touch of her skin against the
bit of his arm that was between the
cupcake case and the butter.

Silver and Fig's eyes boggled.
This was it!

"Stevie are you ready with that ice, love?" Mum's voice came from outside.

Quickly, Stevie pulled her hand away from the butter.

"Coming, Mum!" she called back.

Hurrying now, Stevie grabbed the bowl of ice and tea towel and disappeared out of the door, taking Mama Bo and Daddy Gabriel with her. The cake case still covered the two trembling Twitches, who both let out a huge breath. What a near miss!

"Phew!" said Silver.

"Phew!" said Fig, pulling his arm out of the butter with a big squelch.

Fig slowly licked
the yellow stuff
from his paw.
It didn't taste
quite as good as
he'd imagined,
perhaps because
he was still shaking.

"Thank goodness she didn't spot us.
But we need to be quick! Let's get that
icing and go home," said Silver.

Fig looked at the kitchen clock.
"Um, Silver," he said nervously. "We've
only got fourteen minutes until the
cakes are baked."

They both gulped.

The two rabbits moved fast. The thought of the cake burning, and all the things that might happen if it did, was enough to make them super speedy and soon they were next to the wooden spoon beside the icing bowl. But, they still had to get inside the bowl!

Silver looked about her. Just behind the cake was a pair of lighthouse salt and pepper cellars and some unravelled party streamers.

"I've got it," she said excitedly.
"We're going to make a catapult from
the spoon and that lighthouse salt
cellar. One of us is going to stand on
one end of the spoon while the other
jumps really hard on the other."

Fig was wide-eyed. "How will we
make sure we land in the right place?"

"Oh," said Silver confidently,
thinking of the pages in her favourite
maths book. "It's all about getting the
right angle."

"Couldn't we just climb up the
spoon?"

Silver gave him a frown. "What a

ridiculous suggestion! It would just topple over. Now, do you want to do the jumping-end, or the whizzing-in-the-air-and-landing-in-the-bowl-of-icing-end?"

"Jumping," said Fig immediately. He didn't fancy landing in the wrong place at all. "But how are you going to get out?"

"Before I jump, we'll tie one end of those party streamers to me, and another to you, and you can hold it tight while I climb out."

"Or heave you out," said Fig, warming to the idea.

"Whichever works," said Silver, laughing.

Carefully, the two rabbits pushed over the lighthouse and rolled it into position. Between them they rested the spoon on top, and Silver spent a few moments squinting and frowning, making sure they'd set the angles up right.

Once Silver was sure everything was ready, Fig held the party streamer while Silver tied it tightly around her waist. Then the two rabbits got into position, with Silver standing in the bowl of the spoon, and Fig standing at its tip.

"Don't forget to jump really high and really hard!" said Silver. "After three. One. Two. Three!"

Fig did the biggest jump he possibly could and landed hard on his end of the spoon. As soon as he did, Silver went flying through the air, her long ears flapping in the breeze.

For a moment it looked like she might fly past the bowl, and Fig squeezed his eyes shut. But no, Silver's calculations had been just right. She landed on her bottom with a big squelch, right inside the bowl.

plop...

...splat!

"You did it!" shouted Fig.

"We did it!" shouted Silver. Aware time was running out, she pulled the biscuit jar out of her backpack and began filling it with the sparkly purple icing, right to the very top, as quickly as possible. When it was done, both rabbits looked at the clock.

"Seven minutes," they said at the same time.

Quickly, Silver closed the jar and popped it inside her backpack. Then Fig heaved his end of the party streamer to get Silver out right away.

Heave! Heave! Heave!

In the garden, Nanny Blue was sitting on a garden chair, pressing the bundle of ice against her elbow, and feeling much better, thank you very much.

"We've had enough excitement for one day," said Mum, sighing.

"I haven't had enough excitement!" said Nanny Blue loudly. "More excitement, please!" and everybody laughed.

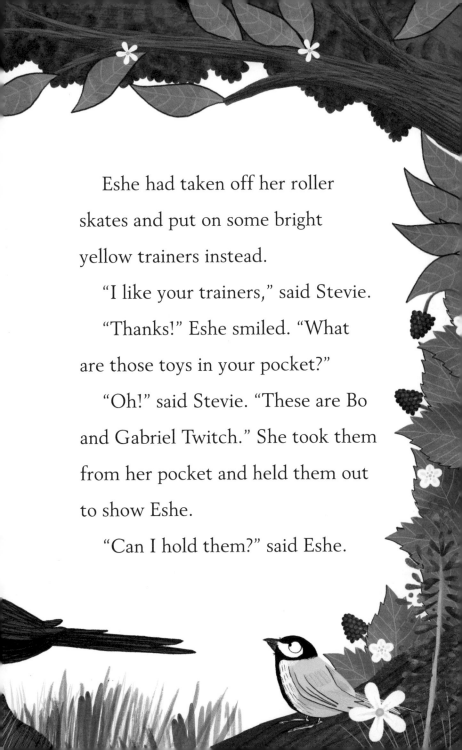

Eshe had taken off her roller
skates and put on some bright
yellow trainers instead.

"I like your trainers," said Stevie.

"Thanks!" Eshe smiled. "What
are those toys in your pocket?"

"Oh!" said Stevie. "These are Bo
and Gabriel Twitch." She took them
from her pocket and held them out
to show Eshe.

"Can I hold them?" said Eshe.

Stevie paused. "Okay," she said, and just like that, she made the decision to trust Eshe with her most treasured possessions. She put the two rabbits into Eshe's open hands.

"Wow, they are gorgeous. I love their little jackets."

Stevie beamed. "I made them."

"You did? That's clever. I like making things too…"

"I'll show you their house after lunch…if you like?"

"Yes please!" said Eshe, passing the two rabbits back to Stevie.

"Everyone! Please go in and help yourself to food," said Mum. "There's a buffet on the kitchen counter. Leave the big cake though." She smiled. "I'll bring that out here for the grand finale!"

"How about you hold Mama Bo, and

I hold Daddy Gabriel?" said Stevie. "And we go and get some food?"

"Thanks!" said Eshe, nodding, and the two girls skipped down the garden together.

Chapter Eight
A Good Day

Inside the kitchen, Fig did one last huge **heave**. Silver pulled herself up onto the rim of the bowl and dropped down onto the counter. Her bottom was covered in icing as she hastily untied the streamer from her waist. They could hear people from outside. Their voices were getting nearer.

"Quick, Fig!" she said. There was no time to lose! The two little rabbits

dashed between the
mountains of food
on the kitchen
counter. They

ran, hopped, jumped,

as fast as they could.
They were almost home,
when something silver
and shiny rolled across
the counter in
front of Fig.

It was

one of the silver

balls Stevie had used to

decorate the cake. Fig leaned

down to pick it up. It was the

size of a Twitch tennis ball. He knew it

would look amazing on top of their cake.

People's voices were getting even

louder.

"Fig! Put it down!" hissed Silver,

who'd made it
to the front door of
the teacup house.

"No!" said Fig. "We need it!"

The people were nearly at the
open kitchen door.

Silver stood with her paws over her
mouth. Fig, now holding the silver ball,
was running towards the teacup house
as fast as he could!

Just as Mum came in, followed by all the other party guests, Fig dived through the front door, and pulled it shut. Another near miss!

"Phew! Made it!" he puffed.

Fig stood up and brushed himself down. "Quick, let's get the cakes out of the oven. The layers should cool quickly, then we can build the cake and cover it in icing."

Together, the two rabbits hid the cakes on wire racks in the little cupboard that Stevie had never really noticed because it looked like it was painted on. Hastily, Silver licked the icing from her paws and wiped it all from her clothes. Fig was just about to tidy away all the little biscuits on the table, where they'd emptied the jar earlier, when he heard a voice.

"This is the teacup house!" said Stevie excitedly from outside. "This is where the Twitches live!"

Silver and Fig stood perfectly still on the tiled floor of the kitchen just as Stevie took the roof off and opened the teacup house. Two big faces appeared above the little rabbits.

"And these are Silver and Fig, the children rabbits," Stevie said.

"Oh, wow!" said Eshe. "They're so perfect!"

Stevie sat Daddy Gabriel next to them. Eshe popped Mama Bo next to them too. The two girls started looking at all the tiny bits of furniture, the little staircase, and the miniature books, pictures, cups and plates. Eshe picked up Silver Twitch.

"This one's got icing on her nose!" said Eshe, giggling.

"How strange," said Stevie, looking down at her fingers. She hadn't even

had any cake, but
Silver very definitely
had some icing on
her nose. How on
earth had it got
there? And why
were the little
biscuits out on
the table? Had

Stevie left them there?

"Oh, wow," said Eshe again, picking
up a miniature shortbread biscuit.
"Look at this toy food. It's so tiny!"

Stevie flicked on the teacup house
lights, so that the inside glowed.

She turned the handle on the pretend
fireplace so that it turned orange like
a real fire.

"This is amazing," said Eshe.

"You'll have to come and play all the
time," said Stevie. "If that's okay, Mum?"

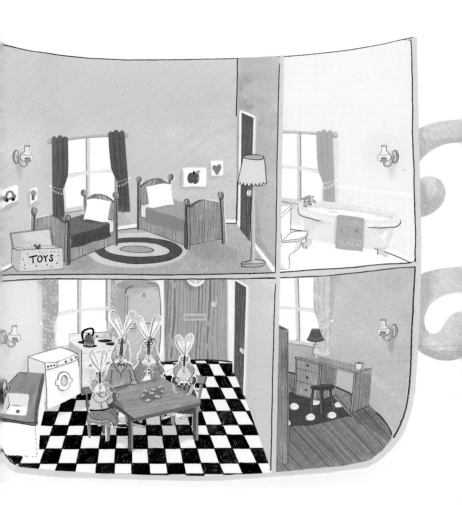

Stevie's mum smiled and nodded as she set out plastic cutlery and people piled the delicious food onto party plates around her. "How about you two get some food and come back and play with the Twitches later? Let's leave them in the house so they don't get all sticky."

Stevie and Eshe looked at each and sighed. They wanted to play with the Twitches now. But Stevie's mum was right. Stevie and Eshe piled up a plate each and began chattering away, about all the things they liked, about school, about how they lived next door to each other, and how brilliant this summer would be. Stevie looked at the sky, at the clouds and the bright sun, and she looked at her new friend and felt happy.

When they were sure they were alone
the Twitches jumped up.

"What on earth have you two been
up to?" said Mama Bo, wiping the icing
away from Silver's nose. "What were
you doing outside the teacup house?"

"Nothing, Mama," said Silver, blushing.

"We made a cake!" Fig said. "Not just any cake. The Purple Party Cake of our dreams. And now we've got to ice it. Quick! Come on!"

Silver reached into the cupboard and brought out the jar of icing and the cake.

"Right!" said Fig. "Who's going to help me decorate it?"

The four Twitches each took a spatula and started to cover the huge cake in purple icing. Each of them pulled their concentration faces, carefully spreading the icing as neatly as possible.

Before they knew it the entire cake was covered and looked AMAZING!

"But where did you get this icing from?" said Mama Bo, frowning. "Not far," said Silver and Fig, giggling as Fig placed the big silver ball right on top.

"It's no laughing matter," began Mama Bo, sternly.

"Now, now, no harm done," said Daddy Gabriel, his tummy grumbling. "Who's for a slice of cake?"

Mama Bo sighed. It was hard to be
cross when such a wonderful cake was
ready to be eaten.

Soon, they were sitting at their little
Twitch table, with slices of the wonderful

cake on little plates, rubbing their

tummies with joy. "This cake is truly

delicious!" said Daddy Gabriel. "You

children really are quite something!"

And nobody could disagree with that.

In the garden, Mum was handing out pieces of her own cake. Stevie and Eshe were sitting next to each other under the fairy lights, each with icing round their faces. "Mum," said Stevie, "do you think I can save up and get some roller skates?"

Mum smiled. "I don't see why not."

"Get some blue ones!" said Nanny Blue, who had icing round her mouth too.

Stevie felt excited. With the Twitches in her life, *and* a new friend, it felt like anything could happen.

Yummy Layer Cake
from Baking for Bunnies

Would YOU love a taste of the Twitches
gigantic purple party cake? This recipe
is a super easy twist on that recipe
for junior bakers to make at home
with the help of a grown-up!

YOU WILL NEED:

FOR THE CAKE:
350g (12oz) softened butter
350g (12oz) caster sugar
6 medium eggs
2 teaspoons vanilla extract
2 teaspoons purple gel food colouring
350g (12oz) self-raising flour

FOR THE BUTTERCREAM:
150g (5oz) softened butter
300g (11oz) icing sugar
3 teaspoons vanilla extract
A little purple gel food colouring

3 x 20cm (8in) sandwich
cake tins and baking parchment

1. Heat the oven to 180°C, 350°F, gas mark 4. Cut a circle of baking parchment to fit the bottom of the tin, then cut two more the same. Grease and line the tins.

2. Put the butter and sugar in a large bowl and mix them together. Beat them with a spoon very quickly until you have a smooth mixture.

3. Break one egg into a jug and beat it with a fork. Mix it into the mixture in the big bowl. Do the same with each of the other eggs. Stir in the vanilla and food colouring.

4. Sift the flour into the bowl. Mix the flour into the eggy mixture very gently, using a metal spoon.

5. Divide the mixture equally between the tins. Smooth the top of the mixture with the back of the spoon.

6. Put the cakes in the oven to bake for 20 minutes.
Poke them with a skewer. If it comes out clean, the cakes are cooked.

When the cakes are cooked, leave them in their tins for 5 minutes. Carefully run a knife around the edge of the inside of the tin. Turn the tins upside down over a wire rack. The cakes will pop out. Leave them to cool.

7. Meanwhile, make the buttercream. Put 150g of softened butter in a bowl, and beat until it is soft and fluffy – like a rabbit's tail!

8. Sift in half the icing sugar and stir it in. Then sift on the rest of the icing sugar and add the vanilla and a little of the food colouring. Mix well. If you would like your icing to be more purple, add more food colouring.

9. Take one of the big cakes with the flat side up and place it on a serving plate. Spread the buttercream over it. Put the other cake on top, flat side down, and spread the buttercream over that. Finally, add the third cake on top and spread over the last of the buttercream.

Your very own purple party cake
is now ready to eat!
Yum!

Fig did this ➜

NO I
didN't!

Meet the Twitches
in their very first adventure!

Meet the Twitches,
four tiny toy rabbits who
live inside a Teacup House.

They belong to a girl called Stevie
and she loves playing with them. But
guess what? These toy rabbits have
a secret. They come alive when
Stevie isn't looking!

Open up the Teacup House – and meet
four little rabbit heroes with big ideas!

ISBN 9781474928120
www.usborne.com/fiction

TEACUP HOUSE

Meet the Twitches

By **Hayley Scott** ❋ Illustrated by **Pippa Curnick** ❋

Look out for the Twitches's next Teacup House story!

The teacup house is
turned upside down when
a bouncy puppy comes to stay at
Stevie's. Scared by the puppy, Silver
and Mama Bo hide in the garden...
and meet a blackbird whose home
also needs protecting.

Open up the Teacup House – and meet
four little rabbit heroes with big ideas!

ISBN 9781474928144
www.usborne.com/fiction

Meet the Author

When Hayley Scott was little, she used to make tiny furniture for fairy houses, placing it in scooped out hollows in her back garden. Today, Hayley lives in Norfolk and still loves tiny things. *Teacup House* is her debut series for young readers.

Meet the Illustrator

Pippa Curnick is an illustrator, designer, bookworm and bunny owner. She gets her inspiration from walking in the woods in Derbyshire, where she lives with her partner and their son.

Look out for more Teacup House adventures, coming soon from Hayley and Pippa!

For Nell with love, always.
And to Alice, Keris
and Rachael. Because. (Hayley)

To Naomi,
with lots of love. (Pippa)

First published in the UK in 2018 by Usborne Publishing Ltd., Usborne House,
83-85 Saffron Hill, London EC1N 8RT, England. www.usborne.com

Text copyright © Hayley Scott, 2018
The right of Hayley Scott to be identified as the author of this work has been asserted by
her in accordance with the Copyright, Designs and Patents Act, 1988.

Illustrations copyright © Usborne Publishing Ltd., 2018
Illustrations by Pippa Curnick.

The name Usborne and the devices ♀ ⊕ are Trade Marks of Usborne Publishing Ltd.

A CIP catalogue record for this book is available from the British Library.

JF AMJJASOND/18

ISBN 9781474928137 04366/1
Printed in China.